"In his latest masterpiece, *A Possum's Patriotic Fourth of July*, Jamey M. Long entertains and enriches our senses though Opie's curious nature and love of laughter, food, and celebration, while Opie is led on an inspiring journey back to the boy's home where he learns about the tragedy, trials, and tribulations endured by the American people in their struggle for freedom and independence. Jamey, through a smart and curious possum that captivates the imagination, teaches us a valuable lesson about how precious freedom truly is and reinforces the importance of celebrating life and family and acknowledging the freedom we so often take for granted. *A Possum's Patriotic Fourth of July* is a carefully crafted tribute to the history of the United States of America that reminds us of the strong beliefs on which the United States was founded. Readers of all ages will enjoy Opie's patriotic adventure and will be captivated by the powerful message of the American people's struggle and victory, which is a true testament that all things are possible through Him."

-Melissa D. Reedy

A Possum's

PATRIOTIC
FOURTH OF JULY

A Possum's

PATRIOTIC
FOURTH OF JULY

written by
JAMEY M. LONG

TATE PUBLISHING & *Enterprises*

Published by Tate Publishing & Enterprises, LLC
127 E. Trade Center Terrace | Mustang, Oklahoma 73064 USA
1.888.361.9473 | www.tatepublishing.com

Tate Publishing is committed to excellence in the publishing industry. The company reflects the philosophy established by the founders, based on Psalm 68:11,
"The Lord gave the word and great was the company of those who published it."

Book design copyright © 2008 by Tate Publishing, LLC. All rights reserved.
Cover design & Interior design by Janae J. Glass
Illustration by Brandon Wood

Published in the United States of America

ISBN: 978-1-60604-974-7
1. Youth & Children: Seasonal

08.07.14

This book is dedicated to all of the brave people who have served or given their lives to protect and build the United States of America. It is these individuals who have helped make this country great. Thank you for all that you have done.

On the edge of a small northern town, there was a forest. It was a warm summer morning, and the sun was shining through the trees. A possum named Opie was happily scurrying through the forest. He was having a fun time climbing the bright green trees and swinging high above the ground by his long, pink tail. As Opie was swinging from the trees, he thought about what a nice day it was and decided to go on an adventure. Walking through the forest was one of his favorite things to do.

As Opie walked through the forest, he could hear in the distance children laughing and people having a good time. *It sounds like someone is having a good time,* thought Opie. *I wonder if it is the boy and his family. They are always doing something fun.* Opie decided to follow the sounds of laughter through the forest. He continued walking until he was at the edge of the trees and could see the boy's backyard. Opie hid behind some of the high grass in the yard and could see the boy and his family and friends laughing and having a good time.

The children and their parents were sitting around a picnic table, while the boy's dad was cooking hotdogs and hamburgers on the grill. The picnic table was decorated with a red, white, and blue tablecloth. There were stars scattered all over, and there was even a bald eagle and a Liberty Bell statue sitting in the center of the table. The boy and some of his friends were all running around the backyard chasing each other with sparklers and were also holding American flags.

I wonder what is going on here, thought Opie to himself, *everything looks so pretty, and everyone is having a wonderful time. The boy and his family are always celebrating something*

important. What could be so special about today? Opie was a very curious possum and loved to laugh and have a good time. He just had to know what was going on. Opie stood up on his hind legs, put his furry nose in the air, and took a great big *sniff!* He smelled the delicious hotdogs and hamburgers. Opie loved food just as much as he loved to laugh and have a good time. Opie wanted to move closer to the boy and the picnic table. He quickly scurried

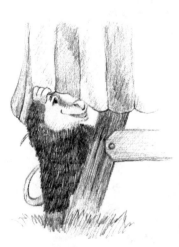 across the backyard and hid underneath the picnic table without being seen by anyone.

Opie could hear the boy talking to his family about *Independence Day,* the *Declaration of*

Independence, and the *Star Spangled Banner*. Opie was known for being a smart possum, but he had never heard of these things before. *What is an Independence Day or a Declaration of Independence,* thought a confused Opie. Opie poked his head out from underneath the picnic table to see if he could figure this all out. Just then, a bright light shown down from above and Opie heard a familiar voice.

"Hello, Opie," said the Voice.

"Hello," replied Opie as he looked up into the bright light.

"I see you have come to celebrate the Fourth of July with the boy and his family," said the Voice.

"I came to visit the boy," Opie responded, "but I do not know anything about the Fourth of July. Is it another holiday?"

"Yes," said the gentle Voice, "the Fourth of July is a holiday. However, it is also much more. The Fourth of July is the celebration of America and its Independence."

"Is the Fourth of July America's birthday?" asked Opie.

"Yes," replied the Voice, "in a way it is. America is over two hundred and thirty years old."

"That is old," replied an amazed Opie. "How did America celebrate its first birthday? And how does it fit all of those candles on the cake?"

The Voice laughed. "That is a good story," replied the gentle Voice. "I am glad you asked.

"I cannot wait to hear it," said a wide-eyed Opie.

"It all started back in the 1700s," the Voice began. "The British, French, and American Indians were all fighting with each other over the land in North America. These battles became known as the French and Indian Wars."

"While these wars were going on," continued the Voice, "there were some people in England who had decided to travel to America. They were looking for a fresh start away from the rule of King George III. These people left England so they could have their own land and work. A lot of people also left England so they could be free to worship me in their own way."

"Those people were very brave," said Opie. "It must have been hard for them to leave their homes to start a new life in a place where they had never seen."

"It was very hard for them," replied the Voice. "Many of them struggled to survive with the few resources that they had to use. After a while, the people in America settled down and divided into thirteen colonies."

"What were the thirteen colonies?" asked Opie.

"The thirteen colonies were divided into three sections," replied the Voice. "The New England colonies were made up of New Hampshire, Massachusetts, Rhode Island, and Connecticut. The people there mostly worked as merchants, anglers, and shipbuilders. These people were really industrious and made things for the other colonies. The people in the middle colonies lived in New York, Pennsylvania, New Jersey, and Delaware. They were primarily farmers. They grew food for the other colonies to eat. The people in the southern colonies lived in Maryland, Virginia, North Carolina, South Carolina, and Georgia. They lived on plantations and grew rice and tobacco that they traded with the other colonies.

"The colonies prospered from their natural resources. Each of the colonies worked with the other colonies and were able to support themselves. They relied on nothing more than the natural resources of wood, rich soil, fish, and the wildlife in the forests that nature offered them to start their new life in America."

"Did King George III help out the people in America?" asked Opie. "That would have been the nice thing to do."

"Actually," said the Voice, "King George III did not help the people, now called colonists, in America. Instead, he and the British Parliament, the British government, taxed the American colonies to pay for the war with the French and American Indians."

"How could he do that?" asked a confused Opie. "That is unfair to the settlers in America who already were struggling to survive."

"That is exactly what the colonists thought too," the gentle Voice responded.

"The colonists said that King George III was taxing them without representation."

"Did King George III take back the tax?" asked Opie.

"No," replied the Voice, "this made the colonists very upset with Britain. To make things worse, in 1765 Britain passed the Stamp Act. King George III said the colonists now had to buy a tax stamp to put on all of their printed documents. This included newspapers, letters, and other important documents.

"This became very expensive for the colonists, and they did not have much money," continued the Voice. "The colonists thought that this was unfair, and they rebelled against Britain. They refused to pay the tax. These rebels were called Patriots, and they were famous for wearing blue coats. There were more colonists becoming Patriots everyday."

Opie looked very sad. "It is too bad that they could not learn to get along with each other," said Opie. "Hopefully King George III learned his lesson and the Patriots and the British were able to get along with each other."

"That would have been nice," said the gentle Voice, "but that did not happen. Instead, in 1770, there was the Boston Massacre."

"The Boston Massacre?" exclaimed Opie. "What is that? It sounds terrible."

"It was," replied the Voice, who was saddened by the tragedy. "In Boston, Massachusetts, a mob of colonists gathered around a British red coat."

"What is a red coat?" asked Opie.

"A red coat is a British soldier," replied the Voice. "They were called red coats because all of the soldiers wore red jackets for their uniform."

"I see," said Opie. "So what happened next?"

"People in the crowd began throwing snowballs at the British soldier," said the Voice. "More British soldiers rushed out to help him, and someone yelled 'Fire.' The British soldiers fired their muskets at the crowd. Five people were killed."

"It is sad when people die," said Opie with a tear in his eye. "The Patriots must have really believed in what they were fighting for."

"Yes, Opie," replied the Voice. "The Patriots strongly believed in having a country of their own. They believed in their cause so much that in 1773 when Britain put a tax on the tea the colonists drank, some of the Patriots fought back."

"What did the Patriots do?" asked Opie.

"The Patriots slipped into some rowboats and rowed out to Boston Harbor where the British ships were docked," explained the Voice. "The Patriots snuck aboard the British ships and dumped all of the tea overboard to protest the tax. Do you know what this event in America's history is called, Opie?"

Opie thought long and hard. "Is it called the Boston Tea Party?" asked Opie.

"Very good," said the gentle Voice. "I am very proud of you. You really are a smart little possum."

"What happened next?" asked a curious Opie.

"In 1774, the delegates met in Philadelphia, Pennsylvania," said the Voice. "It was there that they discussed all of the trouble that was happening in Boston, Massachusetts. This meeting was called the First Continental Congress. Do you know why the First Continental Congress was so important?"

"No, I do not know," said an embarrassed Opie. "But I would like to know."

"That is okay," laughed the Voice. "The First Continental Congress was important because it brought people from the thirteen colonies together to meet as one. It was also there that Patrick Henry said 'I am not a Virginian but an American.' The delegates from the other colonies all agreed and became united as Americans."

"It was also at the First Continental Congress that the colonies formed a militia. The soldiers in the militia were known as Minutemen."

"Let me guess," said Opie, "they were called Minutemen because they were ready to fight in a minute's notice?"

"Very good, Opie," the Voice replied happily. "You are absolutely right. The Minutemen were soon needed.

In 1775, the British soldiers left Boston and headed for Concord, New Hampshire. One of the most famous Minutemen, Paul Revere, saw the British coming. Paul Revere rode out on his horse down the streets yelling 'To Arms! To Arms!' to warn the colonists that the British were fast approaching.

"Thanks to Paul Revere, the Minutemen were ready for the British. They met them in the fields of Lexington," continued the Voice. "There was a battle, and eight Minutemen were killed. The British soldiers began to march onto Concord, but they were soon outnumbered."

"How did the Minutemen outnumber all of those British soldiers?" asked Opie.

"The Minutemen fought and fired their muskets from the trees and forests. The British were only used to fighting battles in straight lines and were unable to see who was attacking them. They were also fighting in a land that they were unfamiliar with. The British realized that they could not win the battle so they retreated. Did you know that it is said that the first shot that began this battle was known as the 'shot heard around the world'?"

"That must have been a really loud shot," said Opie.

"It was, Opie," said the Voice. "The shot let the world know that America was officially at war with Britain."

"If King George was the leader of Britain, then who would lead the Patriots?" asked Opie.

"You are full of good questions," replied the Voice. "The First Continental Congress decided that a man named George Washington, who would become the first President of the United States, would lead the colonial army against Britain. While George Washington was leading his army, the Colonial Congress was meeting in Philadelphia. The delegates, now known as rebels, wanted to be independent from Britain. They decided to write a document that would set America free from Britain and King George III. Opie, do you know what this document was called?"

Opie thought about this and remembered the boy saying something about a Declaration of Independence. *That has to be it,* thought Opie to himself. "Is it the Declaration of Independence?" Opie asked the Voice.

"You are right again," said the Voice.

"You are learning a lot! The Declaration of Independence was written by Thomas Jefferson. It is a very important document. It states that 'all men are created equal.' The Declaration of Independence says that people have the right to life, liberty, and the pursuit of happiness. It also says that government should protect its people and should also respect all of their rights. Finally, it says that if people do not think their government is protecting them, then the people have the right to change it. In 1776, on the Fourth of July, the delegates met in Independence Hall to vote on the Declaration of Independence."

"Did the delegates vote for it?" asked Opie. "I hope they did. It sounds like a wonderful document."

"It is a wonderful document," replied the Voice. "They did vote for it. All of the fifty-six delegates signed it. John Hancock, one of the delegates, signed it really big so King George III could read it without his glasses. After the Declaration of Independence was signed, the people rang the Liberty Bell all day long as a symbol that all of the people in America were united."

"Was this the end of the war?" Opie asked the Voice.

"Unfortunately not," replied the Voice. "The war was not over. In the winter of 1776 on Christmas Eve, George Washington led his army across the Delaware to New Jersey."

"Did George Washington spend Christmas Eve celebrating like the boy does with his family?" asked Opie.

"No, Opie," said the Voice sadly. "There was little celebrating that night. George Washington and his colonial army were fighting the Battle of Trenton."

"There should be no fighting on Christmas

Eve," explained Opie. "There should only be peace and joy."

"You are right," replied the Voice. "There should be no fighting, especially on Christmas. However, the Patriots believed in what they were fighting for, and the war was almost over. In 1777, George Washington was in New York and fought the Battle of Saratoga. Then in 1778, George Washington went to Philadelphia to fight the battle of Valley Forge."

"On October 17, 1781, George Washington and his colonial army finally defeated the British army. General Cornwallis surrendered to George Washington at Yorktown, Virginia. Two years later the Treaty of Paris was signed and ended the American Revolution—"

"—and America was finally free and was a country of its own," finished Opie. "America sure does have a long and brave history that was founded in a strong belief in freedom, religion, and God.""Yes, it does," the Voice spoke to Opie. "America is a wonderful country. It is a land worth celebrating its independence."

As Opie looked around from underneath the picnic table, he noticed that everyone was packing up their things and was heading to the street in front of the boy's house.

"Now, Opie," said the Voice, "it is time for me to leave. If you hurry, you can join the boy and his family for the Fourth of July parade and fireworks."

"A parade and fireworks!" exclaimed an excited Opie. "I love parades and the fireworks. Thank you for teaching me all about the Fourth of July."

"You are welcome," said the kind Voice. "Have a Happy Fourth of July."

"I hope you have a Happy Fourth of July too," replied Opie.

And with that, Opie was off to the parade and fireworks. The boy was standing on the side of the street. Opie spotted a picnic basket sitting next to the boy. He quickly scurried over to it and climbed in. Inside the basket, Opie saw all of the wonderful food. *As long as I am here, I might as well have a snack,* thought Opie. He ate everything in the picnic basket until his furry belly was stuffed full.

After Opie finished eating, he poked his head out of the basket just in time to see the parade and fireworks begin. There were people carrying American flags and singing the *Star Spangled Banner*. There was even a man dressed up like Uncle Sam holding a real bald eagle. Above the parade, the fireworks were exploding into beautiful shades of red, white, and blue.

When the parade was finally over, it was late and the boy and his family went inside to go to bed. *This has been a great day,* thought Opie as he climbed out of the picnic basket, *but I better get back to my home in the forest.* Opie began making his way back home through the forest. Along the way, he proudly carried an American flag in one paw and a sparkler in the other while he sang the Star Spangled Banner. He could not wait to get back home to tell the other animals in the forest about his latest adventure and the history of the United States of America.